THE RUN FOR GOLD

LIFE LESSONS

BY **Michael Caleb Likambi**

Published in the United Kingdom in 2023 by Likambi Global Publishing Ltd

Books by the author:

Tammy and The Shipwreck
Softback: ISBN-13: 978-1-913266-07-3
Rags to Riches
Softback: ISBN-13: 978-1-913266-11-0
The Dreamer
Softback: ISBN-13 978-1-913266-12-7
Wartime
Softback: ISBN-13 978-1-913266-19-6
The Stepbrothers
Softback: ISBN-13 978-1-913266-18-9
The Run for Gold
Softback: ISBN-13: 978-1-913266-22-6

Books by the author:

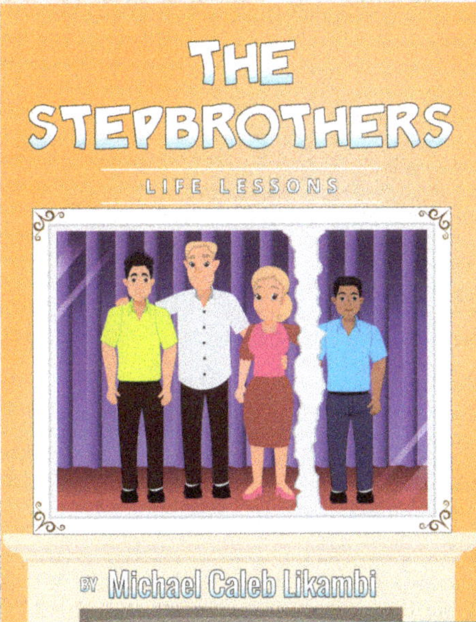

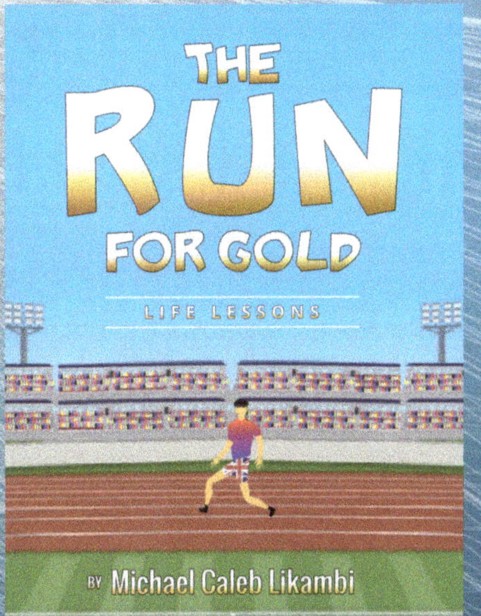

Once upon a time, there was a fat boy named Gordon, who wanted nothing more than to be an Olympic athlete when he was older.

Growing up, Gordon enjoyed watching the Olympics and all the amazing athletes who performed in it. On this particular occasion, while watching the 2012 Olympics, he was greatly inspired by his favourite athlete and role model, Usain Bolt, who was once again the gold medal winner. So one day he decided that he wanted to be an Olympic athlete as well as win a gold medal in a 100m sprint. This dream of his intensified and grew stronger after he watched Usain Bolt effortlessly scoop his third consecutive gold medal in the 2016 Olympics.

There was only one problem… Gordon was always bullied for his weight.

One day he decided to go out and train at the gym, but when he got there a group of bullies approached him. The ring leader was a boy named Brad, who would bully Gordon at school and he would always make Gordon feel insecure.

While he was at the gym, all the boys and Brad were laughing at him because he was going so slow on the treadmill. He then decided to go faster and put the treadmill up to maximum speed, but in the end, he went flying off the treadmill and hurt himself. This only made Brad and his friends bully him even more.

This incident demotivated Gordon, and he stopped working out at the gym. The next day, when Gordon went to school, everyone was talking about what happened to him at the gym while watching the video of him when he fell off the treadmill and laughing. They were all making fun of him.

This made Gordon very upset, so upset that he stopped going to school and spent all his time in his room eating pizza and scrolling through YouTube videos.

One day, while he was at home, his friend sent him a video of how an Olympics trial scout team was coming to school to select children from England to represent them in the Olympics.

NOTICE BOARD

olympics

Chad
Brad
GORDON
Steve

Even though Gordon had not trained for this and wasn't in fit condition, he decided to go and join the competition anyway.

His first race, the hurdles, went quite miserably. He jumped over the first two hurdles with relative ease, but when he came to the third his body gave in and he fell on top of the third hurdle.

He had snapped the hurdles in half and knocked over all the others.

In his second event, he participated in the swimming races. He thought that he would be good in this event as he practised it plenty of times before, but that was years ago. When he jumped in, due to his weight, he started to sink down to the bottom of the pool. Despite his vigorous effort, he couldn't get back up to the surface of the pool.

If the lifeguard hadn't jumped into the pool to help him, he would have drowned. Nobody wanted to make him feel upset, but he could tell everybody was smirking and smiling. The only person who wasn't trying to hide his smile was Brad. He and his friends all laughed and filmed his struggles.

But he decided to not let Brad and his friends get to his head, so he carried on and went to his last event, which was the 700-metre sprint, up and down the hill.

As he took his spot at the start of the race, the starting gun went off. Gordon rushed up the hill as fast as he could, and he successfully ran back down.

On his third time going up the hill, he could feel that his body was giving up but he did not want to admit defeat and be humiliated in front of everyone once again.

So he pushed his body past its limits and when he was running up to the top of the hill on his fifth attempt, he fell back down and started to roll down the hill and knocked over everyone who was running up.

When he woke up, he was in the hospital and his mum was right by his side.

After getting treated, he was soon sent home where he went back to his normal routine of staying inside and sulking in his bedroom.

But one day, while watching a YouTube video, he saw an inspirational video. It was of a woman named Dr Sylvia, and it gave him the motivation to go out and achieve his dream, so he decided to go back out there and do what his heart's desire was.

The next day he went into the gym after a year of not going. It was now an unfamiliar place and many people laughed at him because of his weight and how he looked. He didn't let people's thoughts and opinions put him down because he knew his worth and his goal.

The only thing that put Gordon off was that one of the people who laughed at him was none other than Brad and his friends. He decided to ignore them and grow at his own pace, which is why he went as slow as he possibly could on the treadmill.

Brad and his friends started to laugh at him again, but Gordon had already learnt his lesson and did not let them pressure him into doing something he was not ready for.

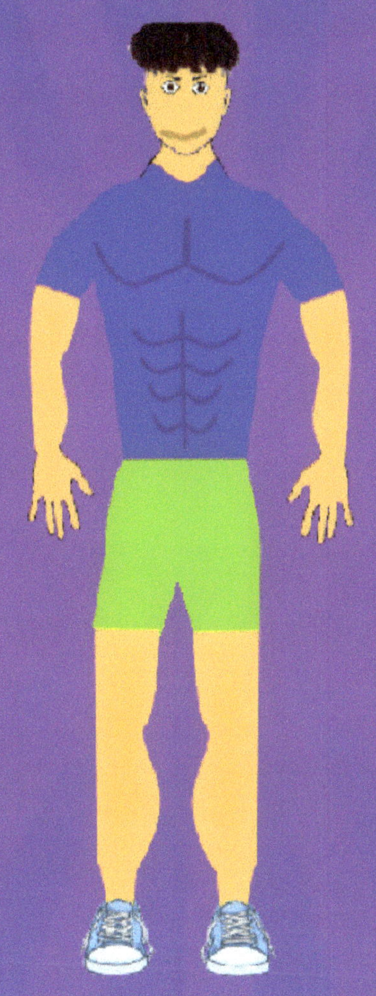

Bit by bit, Gordon started to improve and he was losing weight and gaining muscle as well as confidence. Soon he had an athletic physique and increased his speed to the maximum. He had now beat his personal lifting record and was able to swim faster than he had ever imagined.

It had been a year since the last Olympic event trial, and the talent scouts were coming back to this school. But this time was different, Gordon had trained hard and was now ready. Like the previous year, he signed up for the swimming race, the hurdles, and the 700m sprint. This time he was ready, and he knew things would be different.

He started off with the swimming race; he dived into the pool like an elegant dolphin and sliced through the water like a shark. It looked like he was falling behind but he'd barely begun, he then started to swim faster than everyone there and all the Olympic talent scouts couldn't believe this was the same person from last year! He ended up coming first and beating the person in second place by 10 minutes.

As he got out of the pool everyone cheered him on, even the Scouts congratulated him.

He then warmed up for a second race, the hurdles. This time he took his place and looked at the finish line and set his goals on it. He knew that this was his only chance because he would be too old to take part in the trials the following year. Then the shot for the start of the race went off, Gordon was running past everyone and it was as if he wasn't even looking where the hurdles were; he skipped over them step by step as if they were pebbles. Everyone was amazed and once again surprised that Gordon came in first place.

He was now ready for his final challenge, and this was where he had to prove himself to everyone. In this race, he was up against Brad and some of the most prestigious athletes from different colleges. As soon as the assistant waved his flag, he set off like a rocket.

He was seven laps ahead of everyone and ended up breaking the city's record for the fastest 700 m.

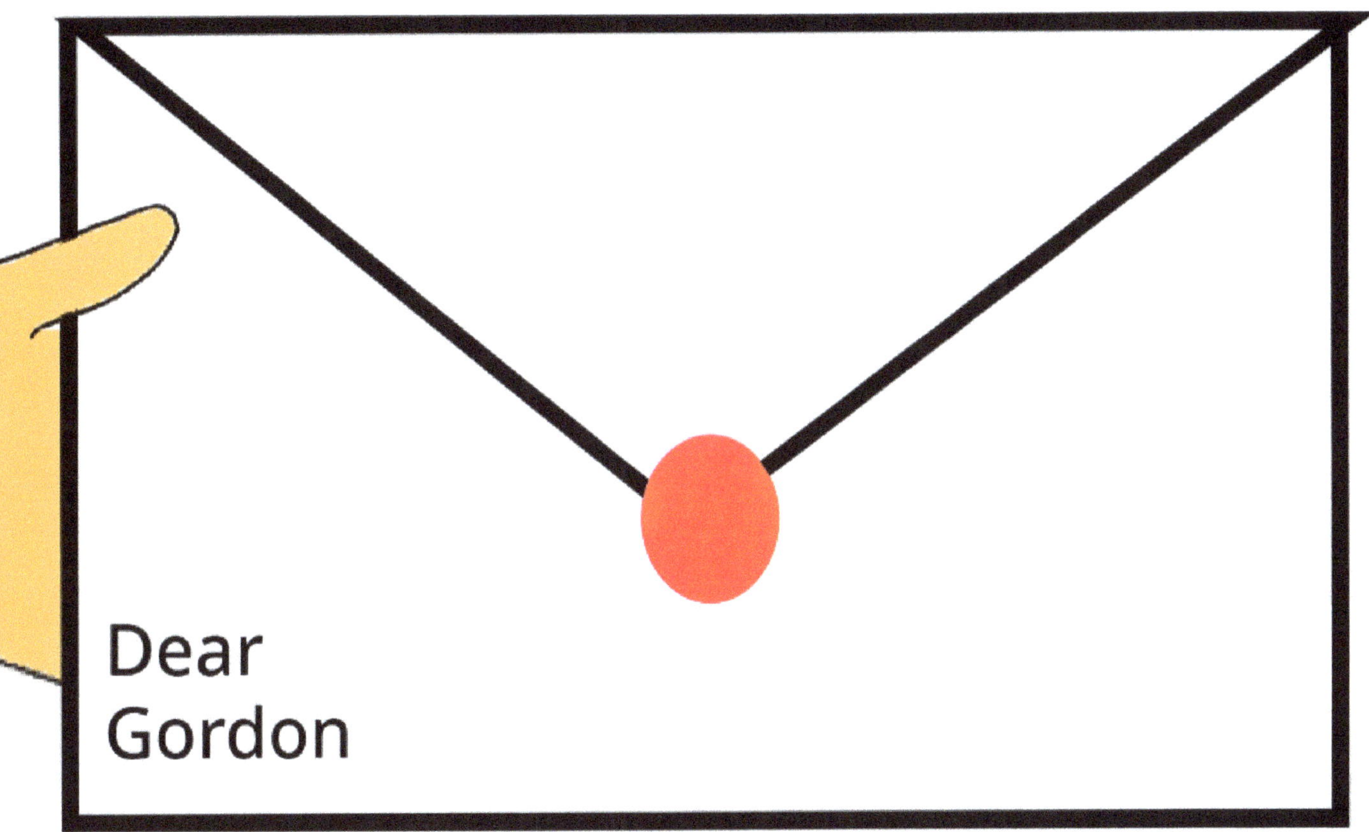

Two days later, he received an envelope at his front door; it was an acceptance letter from the Olympics Training Centre. He jumped up and down with joy and he knew he had worked hard for this. He then packed his bags and two days later, he set off to Paris.

He trained at the Olympics Academy for two years and was finally chosen to represent his country in the Olympics along with Brad. He was chosen to run the 400m sprint and the relay. Building up to this day he had a lot of nerves and when the day finally came, he was doubting whether he could really do it. But then he remembered all those years back and why he decided to turn his life around… He also watched several of Dr Sylvia's inspirational videos again, then he got up and had an eye for the gold.

Then in front of millions of people, his name was called up on the speakers and he got ready for the relay. In the beginning, his team got off to a bad start and they kept on going further behind.

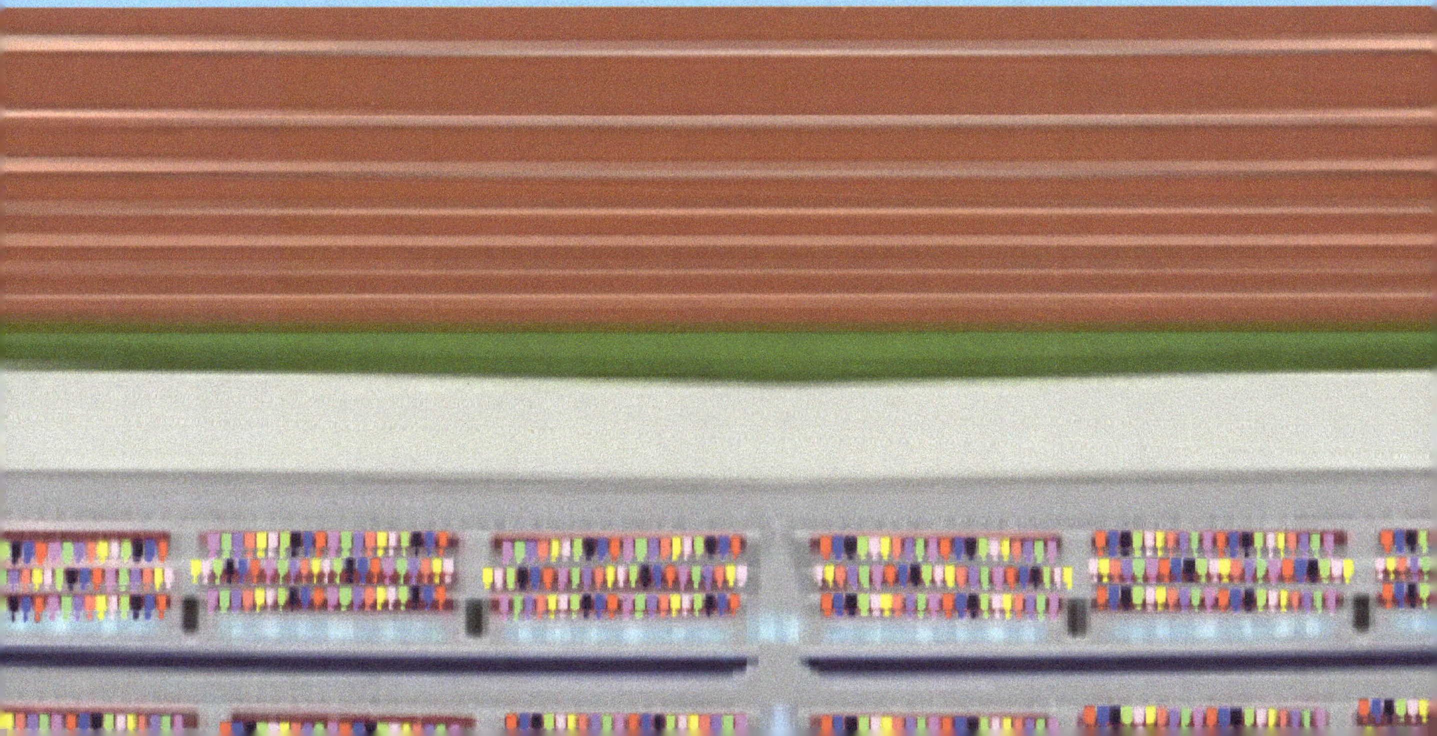

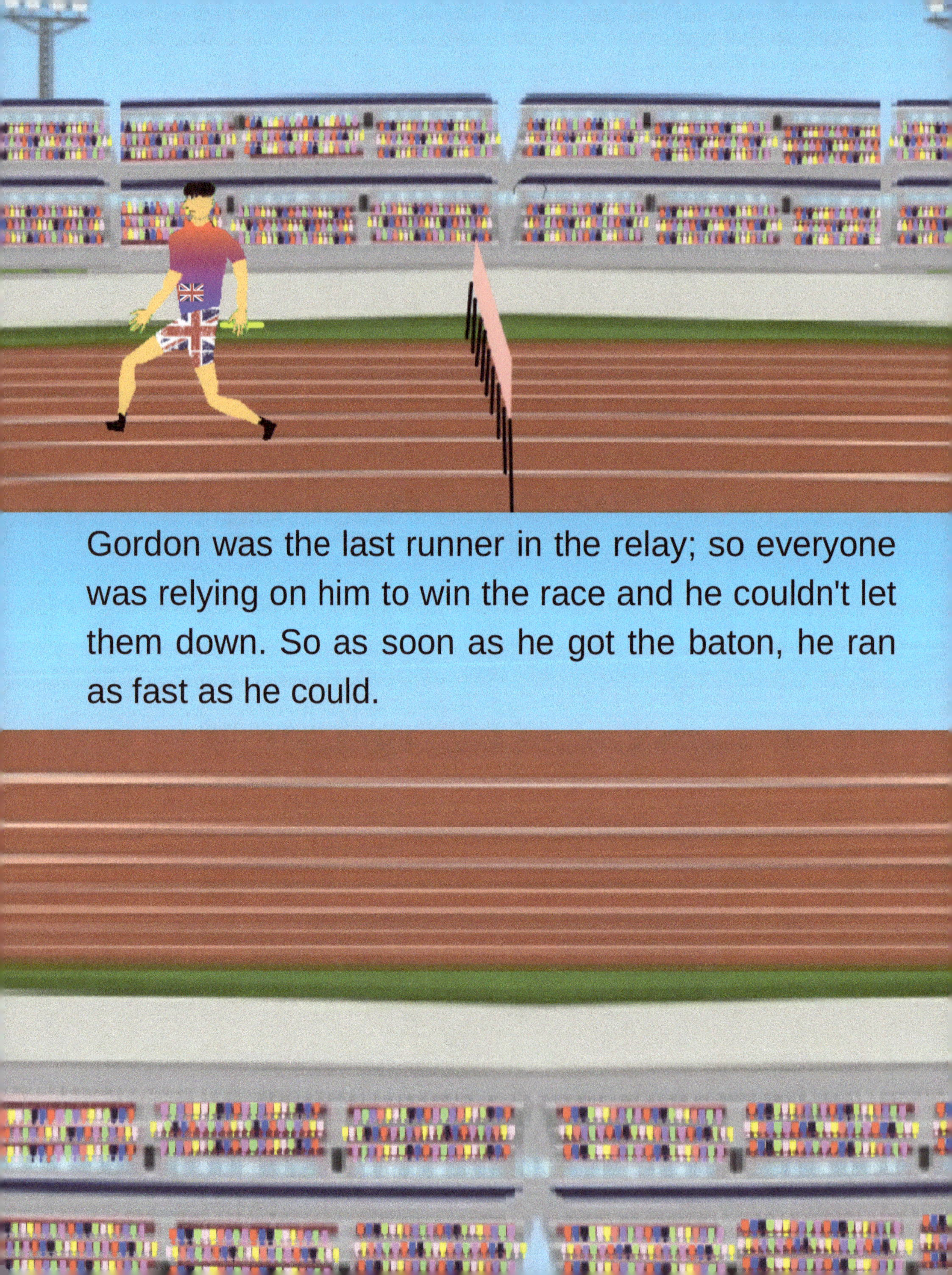

Gordon was the last runner in the relay; so everyone was relying on him to win the race and he couldn't let them down. So as soon as he got the baton, he ran as fast as he could.

He could soon see the finish line in his sight and dashed forward, and then and there his dreams came true.

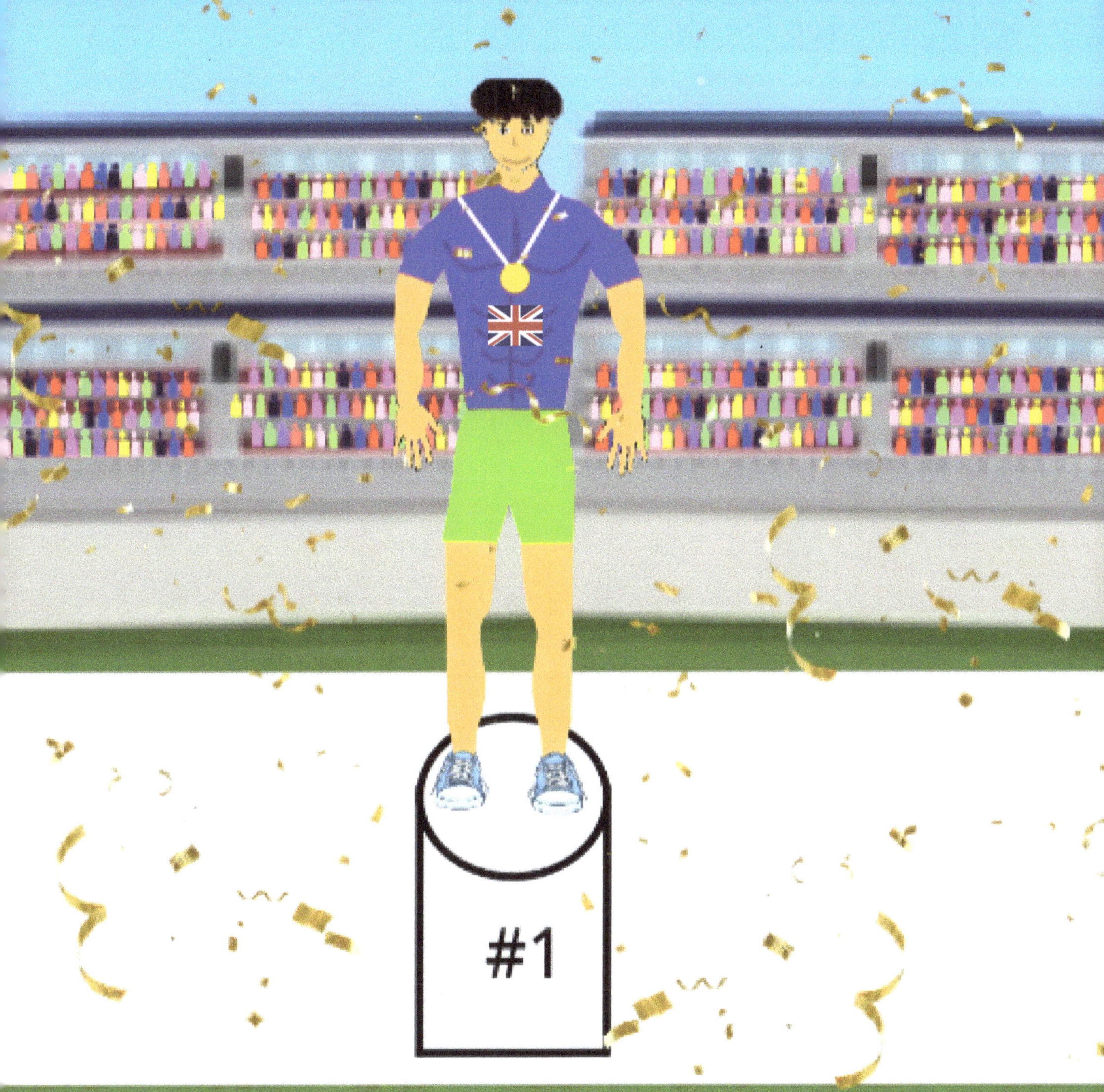

BLURB

"Once upon a time, there was a fat boy called Gordon"...

Come along on an inspiring journey with a young and bright boy named Gordon. Filled to the brim with talent and aspiration, Gordon's golden dream is to be an Olympic champion.

However, throughout his journey, he unfortunately faces bullying, problems and constant cruelty shown towards him due to his weight...

Do you believe that Gordon will run for his gold and chase his dreams? Or will doubt and negativity ambush his vision?...

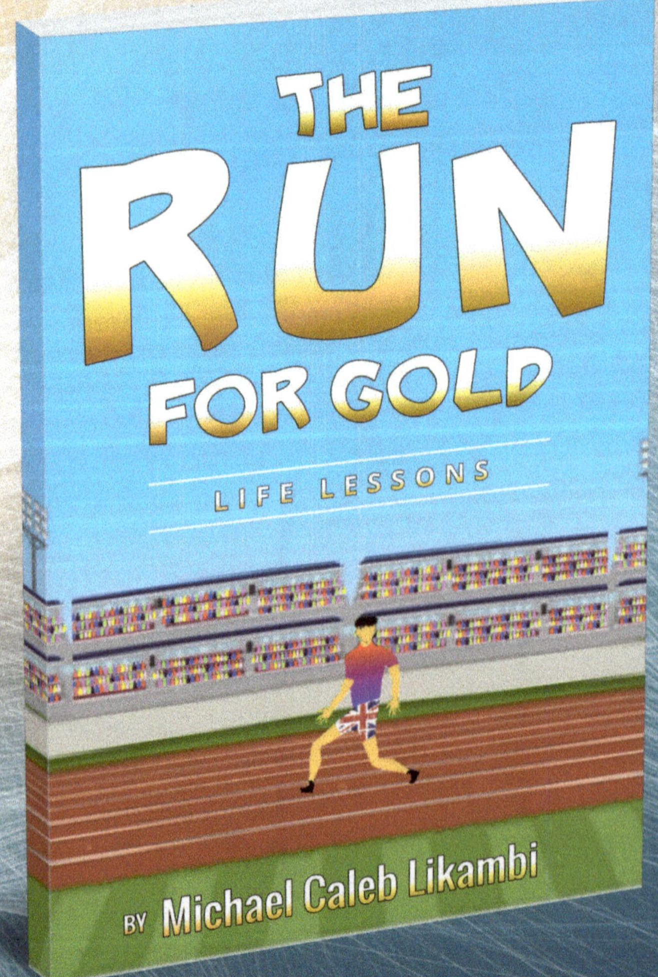

ABOUT THE AUTHOR

MICHAEL CALEB LIKAMBI

"Always surround yourself with people who inspire you to be great, but most importantly, be that person who inspires others to be great." Caleb Likambi

Coming from a family of talented young writers, Michael Caleb Likambi debuted as an author at the age of 12 with his best-selling book, Tammy and the Shipwreck, and in less than a year, he published five books. In August 2023, Caleb wrote and illustrated 10 new books which will be released early next year. The release of these 10 new books is a testament to Caleb's talent and passion for storytelling. He won the William Woodward Prize for Creative Writing at his secondary school this year

Caleb is an ultra-confident and grounded young man, whose kind, compassionate, and humble personality makes him a true friend to many. He always stands up for those who are bullied or mistreated, and he is fondly referred to as the "soft giant." He is a positive role model for children and young people all across the globe.

Caleb has been the Head Boy at his secondary school for three consecutive years and has been on the School Council numerous times throughout his time in primary school. He is also a gifted and natural sportsman, who has won numerous trophies and awards, both as an individual and for his primary and secondary schools.

ABOUT THE AUTHOR

MICHAEL CALEB LIKAMBI

"Reading is such fun. It has the power to expand your imagination and take you into different parts and cultures of the world at the same time."
Caleb Likambi

Caleb's genuine passion for reading and learning is second to none, which goes back to his childhood when he would read until he fell asleep. He's read over 700 books to date and never stops requesting new books. He has been interviewed by and featured on diverse media platforms, including BBC Radio Merseyside and the Liverpool Echo.

Caleb's dedication to sharing his love of reading and writing extends beyond his own books. Together with his siblings, he actively advocates for literacy and education, speaking in schools, libraries, and events and working to make diverse children books accessible to children from all backgrounds. Through his donations to schools and libraries, Caleb hopes to inspire young readers to discover the joy and transformative power of reading.

Caleb and his siblings have received special recognition for their work and have collaborated with diverse libraries and schools across Liverpool to host a series of book tours and events. As a young author, his goal is to create diversity in children's literature and make the books available to young people and inspire as many children as possible to unlock their creative genius and full potential. He is determined to inspire his peers to develop a love for reading and writing, and he wants others to write their own books.

ABOUT THE PUBLISHER

LIKAMBI GLOBAL PUBLISHING

Published by Likambi Global Publishing Ltd.
Email: publishing@likambiglobalpublishing.com
Tel: +44 (0) 7539 216072
www.likambiglobalpublishing.com

We are a Dynamic Family-Led Cutting-Edge Global Publisher set up to simplify and enhance your writing and publishing experience and unique journey to becoming a renowned and confident author.

Whether you are an adult or child, we have a special team that is devoted to working with you throughout your writing and publishing journey with us! All of our consultants and coaches/mentors are bestselling authors with years of hands-on experience and a wealth of knowledge uniquely tailored to meet your individual needs!

Our goal is to provide you with the ultimate writing and publishing experience required to share your unique message and voice as an author with the world and strive to greater heights!

Publications are done three times a year; January, June, and November. All manuscripts must be received at least 90 days prior to publication dates.

OTHER CHILDREN BOOKS BY LIKAMBI GLOBAL PUBLISHING

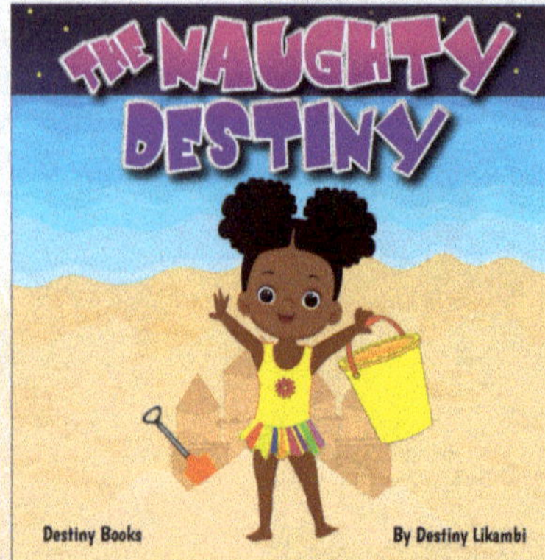

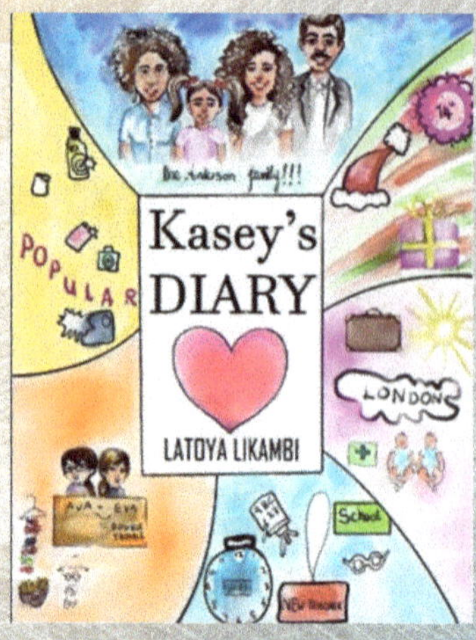

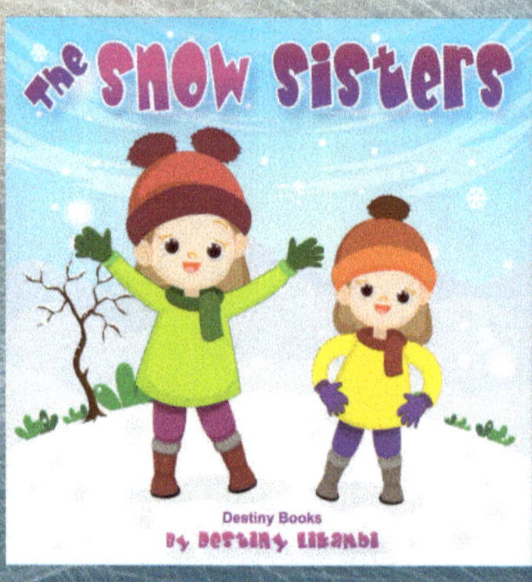

OTHER CHILDREN BOOKS BY LIKAMBI GLOBAL PUBLISHING

The Stepbrothers
Softback: ISBN-13 978-1-913266-18-9

Rags to Riches
Softback: ISBN-13: 978-1-913266-11-0

The Dreamer
Softback: ISBN-13 978-1-913266-12-7

The Naughty Destiny
Softback: ISBN-13: 978-1-913266-13-4

Destiny and The Troll
 Hardback ISBN 13: 978-1-913266-06-6
 Softback ISBN 13: 978-1-913266-05-9

The Girl on The Journey
 Hardback ISBN 13: 978-1-913266-93-6
 Softback ISBN 13: 978-1-913266-94-3

Tammy and the Shipwreck
 Softback ISBN 13: 978-1-913266-07-3

Short Stories by Latoya Likambi
 Softback ISBN 13: 978-1-913266-03-5

Kasey's Diary
 Hardback ISBN 13: 978-1-093291-26-1
 Softback ISBN 13: 978-0-368630-50-7

The Snow Sisters
Softback: ISBN-13 978-1-913266-14-1

Wartime
Softback: ISBN-13 978-1-913266-19-6

Chicky and the Forest
Softback: ISBN-13 978-1-913266-15-8

The Summer Holiday
Softback: ISBN-13 978-1-913266-21-9

The Run for Gold
Softback: ISBN-13: 978-1-913266-22-6

Family Adventure
Softback ISBN 13: 978-1-913266-23-3

Anderson Adventure (Kasey's Diary Book 2)
 Softback ISBN 13: 978-1-913266-99-8

The Babysitter
Softback ISBN-13: 978-1913266974

Books by Michael Caleb Likambi:

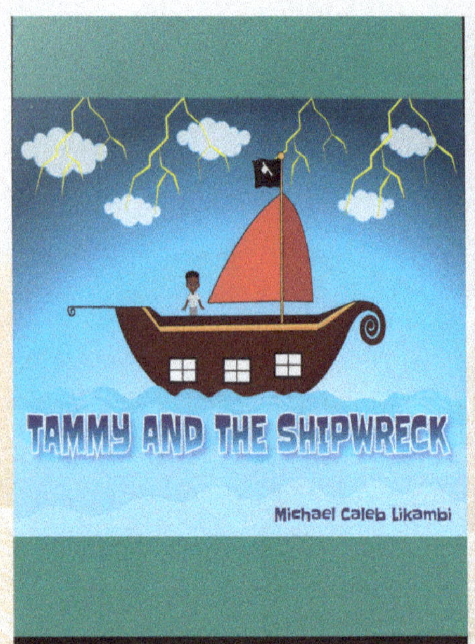

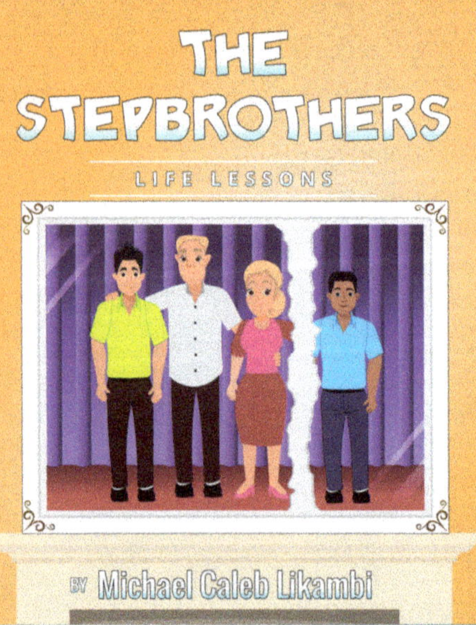

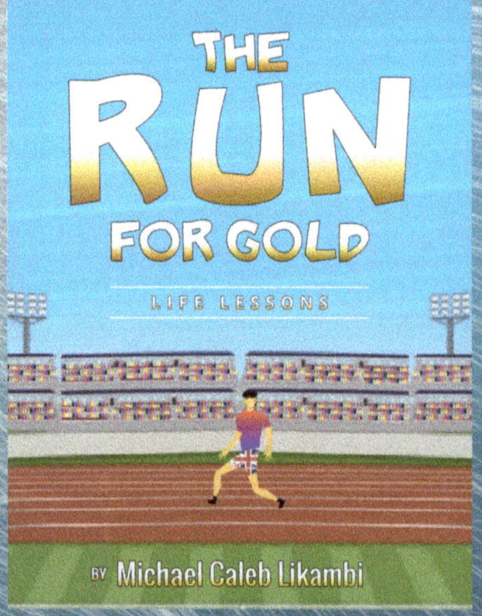

Life Lessons Series by Caleb Likambi:

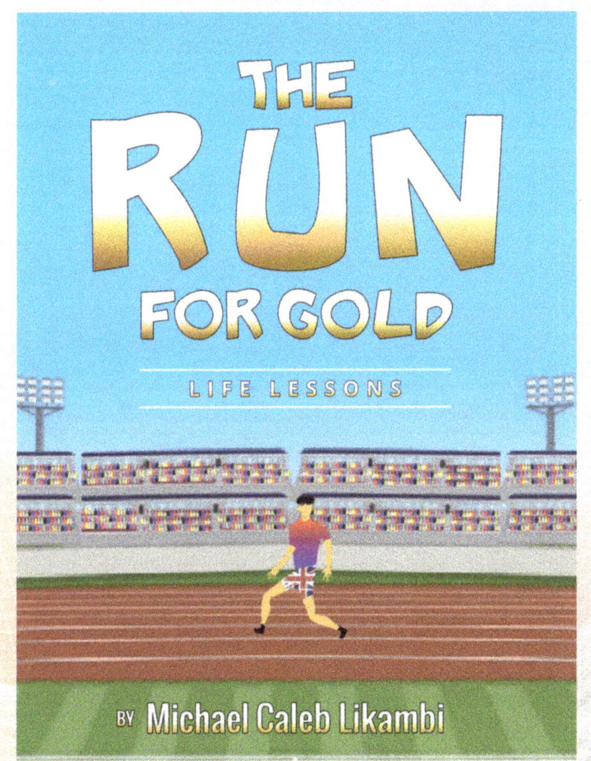